THA COLLECTION

By

Jason Williams Sr.

I Cower in the Corner

I cower in a corner,
Shaking in fear; tears
Fall from my eyes.

I'm just a kid, ten years old,
And I'm shaking,
Scared for my life.

I sit amongst broken dishes
And yells at high pitches
And pray none's directed my way.
I've endured the wrath
Of this man before and I know
This man doesn't play;

Many times I've witnessed
Nights from his drunken binges
Still unsure how this night will end.
I'm guessing with Mom crying,
Wishing he'd die again
When will this nightmare end?

But despite the black eyes
And the degrading names she's called,
She refuses to take me out of this Hell.
So I cower in the corner
Shaking like a leaf, wishing
There was someone I could tell.

I cower in the corner,
A kid fearing grown-ups
Who seem unaware of the repercussions.
The unintended consequences
Their words are inflicting on me,
Because they keep on fussing.
Yet they feel this strife
Is a part of life—I just wish
It wasn't a part of mine.

So I cower in the corner, shaking but keeping quiet,
Hoping they don't notice me crying.

Sitting

Sitting in an alley,
Praying to myself:
Lord, please help me
Out of this situation.
It's cold and it's raining,
I'm alone contemplating:
Will tonight be the night
Of my death?

I have no one to blame
But myself once again,
Because I'm young, dumb

And at times act foolish.
I messed with the wrong people
I thought weren't my equal,
But this time my decision
Seems stupid.
Because there are two Cadillacs
(One brown and one black)
Searching for me now
In the streets.
They're loaded with weapons
(Rifles and Smith and Wessons)
And me out of bullets—
How can I compete?

This day started good
With me out in the 'hood,
Being ignorant,
Playing with fire,
Harassing a whole family
Who suffer from insanity,
Now they all want me
To expire.
I tried to do them all harm,
But they sounded the alarm
Because I missed,
Now they're out to get me.

Now I hide in an alley

Sitting

Cold and shivering badly,
Hoping when they pass
They don't see me.
But they do
They see me (it's kind of like TV)
Because I'm running
To avoid interception.
With my weapon empty
And shells they have plenty,
So I run with no
Source of protection.

But I find a hiding spot
And pray once again:
"Lord, please help me out of this situation."
Because I'm young and dumb
And my cold body is numb—
Then headlights light up
My location.

No Child

No child asks to be brought
Into this world,
But when one is;
That child is a blessing.
Whether planned or not,
That child is loved by God,
So every child is
One of God's blessings.
But there are those who fail
To do what's needed
(To raise that blessing
Up right).
That mother or father
With love to offer
But withhold it because
Of selfish desires.

When that child is born,
No one should do harm,
Whether physically or by
Neglect.
The day that child's conceived,
No parent should retreat
From their responsibility
To protect.
That child, that blessing,
Until the day that person
Is old enough

To be on their own.

So until that child's grown
And leaves your home,
The responsibility for
That child is not for one parent alone:
It's both parents' job,
Not just Mom's or Dad's
It took two to make that life.

No Child

And their job doesn't end
If they're separated
Because of trouble and strife.

Because now you have fathers
Who don't care or bother
With the child when the woman's gone.
You divorce the lady
But not your baby:
To do that is plain wrong.

And then there are women
Who don't raise their children—
They leave them with Grandma or Dad.
Regardless of the reason
For that woman leaving,
The child will harbor negative
Feelings for that.

So each child that is born
Didn't ask to be here,
Let's just make that clear.
They should be loved,
Hugged and protected,
Not longing for parents who
Are not there.

I Live Daily

I live life with a daily
Inspiration, because I know from where I came.
In my short life
I've seen pain,
And endured through hardship
And rain.

Death was never far away
That's why each day
I try to smile.
I never take things
Too seriously; inside of me
There lives a child.
Who plays and enjoys
Life to its fullest
Because tomorrow's not guaranteed.

If you've been where I've been
And seen what I've seen,
You'd understand what I mean.
Old friends are gone:
God called them home
(Almost all at an early age).

And yet I still live—
What a blessing that is
So I cherish each and every day.

I take nothing for granted
Inside of me is planted
A will that presses me on.
Because my past is gone
I aim to stay strong
Until God calls me home.

What Has Man Done?

Man has separated the church
Based on different
Bible verses.
You can see it riding
Down the street
Based on the different-named churches.

Jesus wants his children
Together and not
Separated by different walls;
He wants his children
United and not divided—
For that, man is the cause.

The Bible says: Come as you are
And allow him to change you
From within.
Come together under Jesus Christ
And not separate because of man.

Men have taken God's word
And used it to separate themselves;
They've created different doctrines,
And most think the others are
Going to Hell.

But how strong would
The church be
If all Christians came together?
We could spread God's teaching
And influence others to seek Him better.

Christianity would spread like wildfire
All across the earth;
Everyone would hear the
Message of Jesus Christ
And his church.

So while we bicker
Because of petty differences,

What Has Man Done?

We lose unbelievers.
How strong would we be
If we were all united

Under our Savior, Christ Jesus?

The Conversation
Mother=M
Son=S
Police=P

M: I think we need to talk, Son,
Because you are living wild,
And I want the best for you
Because you're my only child.

S: But, Mom, I'm just having fun,
Being young, sowing my oats;
I just need to get it out of my system
Before I get old.

M: Son, tomorrow is not guaranteed
And you're living fancy-free;
AIDS is real, so is Hell—
Do you understand me?

S: Mom, I won't get AIDS,
I use protection every day.
And I know about Jesus
But I don't wanna be saved,
Because then I can't go to the clubs,
And get drunk.
Mom, I'm just a kid
And I only want to have fun.

M: Son, Jesus
Laid down his life
For you and me,
Because he wants you to be
In Heaven for eternity.
And, Son, condoms break—
That's why you are here today.
Getting drunk all the time,
You're throwing your life away.
Son, if you die today,
Do you know where you will be?
Will you be in Hell,
Burning for eternity?

The Conversation
Mother=M
Son=S
Police=P

Or will you be with him,
He who loves you with all his heart?
I can't make the decision for you, Son,
It's your choice.

S: Mom, I understand what you're saying,
But I'm old enough,
To make my own decisions
I'm not giving up my liquor.
And I'm not giving up women
Right now I'm gonna keep on sinning,
But I will turn my life over
When I turn twenty.
Mom, I do love you,
But I'm late for another date;

And if you're worried about my soul,
Then, Momma, pray.

M: Lord, please protect my baby
While he's on the street,
Shelter him with your love
Because it's you he really needs.
Please be his armor, Lord.
Please be his shield, Lord.
I know that his head is hard—
The Devil is a lie, and
I give him up to you, Lord.

Tick tock
Tick tock
Tick tock
Tick tock

(Later that night)

Ring! Ring!

The Conversation
Mother=M
Son=S
Police=P

M: Yes, can I help you?
Who's calling me at two?

P: Ma'am, its Officer Johnson
From station house twenty-two.

M: Oh, Lord, what has happened?
Is my son in trouble again?
Do I have to come and bail
My son out once again?

P: Ma'am, I'm so sorry to
Tell you—your son is deceased.
He had a wreck.
They pronounced him dead
On the street.
We need you to come down
To the station
And fill out some papers,
Because your son was driving drunk
And he ran over a lady,

And she died at the scene
I know this is like a bad dream,
But I need you to come down
And claim your son's things.

M: Oh, Lord, my son!
He was just a baby!
Oh, Lord! Oh, Lord! Oh, Lord!
My baby!!!!!!

Take Heart

Take heart,
For you are great
And more talented than you believe.
Your ability is only stifled
By what your mind believes you can achieve.
For your abilities to shine
And your goals to come into fruition,
It starts with your thinking
Because from one's mind comes ambition.

What a man think, so he is:
For right now, let that sink in.
If a man thinks he is untalented
Then untalented he is.
But knowing in your mind
Any hill you climb you can reach the top—
You just have to be mentally prepared
With a right mind and don't stop.

Take heart,
For what you think of yourself
Can be seen in your actions;
It can be heard in the words you speak
Because from one's mouth comes one's passion.
If your mind is right and you're dedicated
To doing what it takes to succeed,
You'll spend your time, your energy, your sweat
Achieving what you believe.
Your hands will work daily toward
The task that is needed to accomplish your goals.
As your mind and actions work jointly,
You'll watch as your dreams unfold.

Take heart,
For your heart must be right,

Along with your mind and your actions.
Honesty and goodness need to dwell
Inside your whole heart, not just a fraction,
And rightness needs to abide
Inside of this most important muscle.

Take Heart

Where good and evil fight daily
But love succeeds against all tussles.

If one's heart is content with his situation
In life, it'll show.
His time will be spent not constructively
But instead pursuing the status quo.
So your heart, mind and actions
Need to work together to succeed;
And with God as your pilot,
Which is also vital, you will succeed.

Stand Up

Who among us will stand up
And decry the language of our oppressors,
The words that were meant
To depress us
And single us out like lepers?

Who among us will stand up
And stop calling our black queens
Female dogs
And educate our sisters
From screaming, "That's my song!"
When it degrades them,
Berates them and depicts them all wrong?

Who among us will stand up
To negative videos and TV shows
That depict us as thugs, hoochies and ho's.
Shows that fail to educate,
But instead propagate,
Violence and negative stereotypes
In which we're supposed to relate?

Who among us will stand up
And show our young ladies how to dress,
Teach them that perception can damage
Success,
And that their mind is their most
Valuable asset?

Who among us will stand up
And teach our black males respect—
Respect for our communities and families
And the opposite sex;
Respect for our past and present
And our destination;
Respect and reverence for God,
Our soul creator?

Who among us will stand up
And proclaim as a mother and father,
Sister, brother,

Stand Up

That my family will survive
Despite any and all trouble?

Who among us will stand up

And declare that our sons
Will not end up in jail?
And that no one will impregnate
Our young, black, underage females;
And, despite our careers
And every pressing matter in which we engage,
That we, as African Americans,
Take time, make time,
To make sure our kids serve no time!

I among us have stood up
To break every metal chain to success
That comes my child's way;
I have stood up
To teach my child proper dress,
Proper speech and what not to say.

Who else among us will stand up?

No More

She sat on her bed
Feeling sadness and shame,
'Cause she believed him
When he said it wouldn't happen again.
"But he's said this before and, once again, he lied,"
Is what she said to herself as she rubbed her blackened eye.
But this time she would leave him:
"No more, I'm finished."
But she said this before
And still stayed with him.

She packed up her bags

And cried all the while,
And thought to herself,
"I can't separate this man from his child."
So she started packing slowly,
Then eventually stopped.
She sat on her bed
And uncontrollably sobbed.

She thought to herself,
"I have nowhere to go;
My family would just laugh
And say I told you so.
I can go to my friends
But why? This is my house,
And instead of me leaving,
He should get out;
He's the one who hit me
And after all we've been through."
So she picked up the phone
And told him she's done, they're through.

He cursed her and threatened her
And said when he got home
He'd make her regret
Calling him on the phone.
She hung up, now frightened;
She knew what that meant.
So she picked up the phone and called the police.

No More

They came and took pictures,
Picked him up from his job;
Now there's peace in her house
Since the violence has stopped.

My Mother

Do I, in my everyday actions,
Endeavor to make my mother proud?
Whether standing before me
Or looking, do I make
My mother smile?
When my name's spoken
In her presence, does her heart
Jump for joy?
Or does she feel sadness
Because the life she gave
I am now trying to destroy?

Am I what my mother saw in me
The day I left her womb,
The day I opened my eyes
And wiggled my toes?
Am I the same person she's groomed,
To be respectful and respecting
Of all people, despite his or her beliefs,
To put God first and family second
While giving back to the community?

Or am I selfish and conceited and think
Everything is about me?
Do I make her feel happiness
Or regret at night before she falls asleep?
Or does she feel like a failure

When I act rebellious,
Forgetting everything's she's taught?
Do I make her day brighter,
Looks forward to my arrival,
Or instead think to herself, "Child, get lost"?

Am I a correct representation
Of the values that were placed in
Me from years of conversation.
From eighteen years of her telling me
What's best for me,
Loving me and showing patience?
But now in my older age,
Am I at a different stage in life

My Mother

To where I show disrespect,
Using foul language
In front of the woman
Who tried to teach me respect?

So the question I ask myself
Is the question you should ask:
Does my mom walk
With her head held high,
Or does she still have to tell me,
"Stop being rebellious:
Be respectful and reach for the sky"?
Do I make my
Mother proud?

His Dad

He didn't say a word
As he opened the casket
And he could finally see his face.
He looked down at the man
He sometimes called Dad,
Who finally sealed his own fate.
It's not that he didn't love him,
He just didn't respect him,
And now he only felt grief
That this man he called Father
Didn't try or bother
With being the best dad he could be.

But now it's in the past
Because his dad is deceased,
And after today, never again will he hear,
"Son, I will do better"
In person or in letters.
His pain ends, without tears,.
So he looks at the ceiling,
Ashamed because he's feeling
No longer grief but peace for this man.

Because his life has been hard,
His journey unstable,
He never has to fight again.
He never has to spend
More nights in prison—
No longer is that a concern.
He looks back down at his dad
And lets one tear fall:
"Rest in peace, 'cause peace you deserve."

Have I Failed?

Have I failed in my efforts
To raise a decent human being,
Because he stands on the
Other side of a cell in front of me?
Did I not give him enough love
Or enough hugs;
Did I not say "I love you"
To him every day just because?
Did I not teach him
That for any crime there's consequence,
That there's right and wrong,
No one straddles the fence?
But him being incarcerated
Is at least minor evidence,
That he either failed to listen
Or understand exactly what I meant.

Have I failed in my efforts
To raise a decent human being,
'Cause now a number
Replaces his name as his identity?
If I could have seen his future
In his eyes when he was born,
What steps could I have taken,
What difference could I have done—
Move to another neighborhood
And lock my son inside,
Hoping and praying that from his future
He could hide?
Or take him to church more
And pray, pray, pray?
Or tell him his future will consist
Of being locked away?

Have I failed in my efforts
To raise a decent human being,
In his eyes, as a child
I saw no hint of wrong-doing.
But yet, as an adult,
My child's stuck in the system,
Eyes pleading for help,

Have I Failed?

While behind bars it hurts but I listen.
In my state of grief
Where's my peace?

Because in my sons eyes, there's pain,
But there's no release;
Because of his crime, a debt
Has to be paid.
Even though it hurt
Each day when I remember
My son is in a cage.
I remind my son
The battle's not over
No matter what anyone says.

So I have not failed
In my effort to raise
A decent human being:
Despite what he's done,
He still is my son,
And forever he will
Be a black king.

God Loves Us

No matter your color,
Your creed or your nationality,
God loves us all the same—
Despite our status or salary.

Though some feel that God's light
Only shines in their life,
His light shines on us all,
Despite our troubles and strife.
And though darkness comes,
It only stays for a while;

Problems come to the just
And unjust, it's temporary, so smile.

Another reason to be joyful
Is that you opened your eyes
This morning when you awoke
And greeted the sunrise.
He shines on our life
Despite the clouds overhead,
And despite our imperfections,
He's always done what He's said.

To those who accept His mercy
And let Him abide in their heart,
He will walk with you daily
And from you He will not depart.

So no matter your color, your creed
Or nationality, God loves us all the same—
Despite our status or salary.

Forces Unseen

Though we battle forces unseen,
Forces that come to stifle our dreams.
And influence our children
To walk not in light,
So it's our job as parents
To teach our kids right.
And not only to tell them
But show it to them daily.
So when the devil comes
And tries to make you crazy
With problems and worries,
We should watch what we say,
Because our kids are watching
What we say anyway.

They listen for words
And negative phrases,
So when you tell them, "Don't curse!"

They won't say they heard you say it,
Yet they won't say a word
When you go into a rage—
They just see you're not living
The life that you say.
So instead of fussing and cussing
When inside anger builds,
Just say a silent prayer
In the presence of your kids.

And they watch our actions
And they know when we slip;
In church we're one way
But at home the opposite.
At church we are tithers,
We pray and we shout;
But when church is over
We're quick to curse someone out.
At church we are friendly,
We love everyone,
But we fail to show patience
With our daughters and sons.

Forces Unseen

We say: "Love everyone
Because we are God's children,
But don't trust those people
Because their skin is different."
And we tell them to get married
And for God's words show passion,
But we fail to live it—
It shows because we're shacking.
Or say no to drugs,
For your body show respect;
But when we get a chance,
We light up a cigarette.

We battle influences,
Like cable and B.E.T.,
Who spend billions of dollars
To control what our kids see.
But despite what they spend,
Inside of us there's One greater than all;
So when Satan comes knocking,
Teach your kids who to call.

Destination

On this day of the month,
I pray for God's mercy,
That traffic this day is light.
I pray That everyone's safe
And no one has to wait,
I pray no one has a wreck and dies.
I pray for sanity.
For everyone who is driving,
I pray they arrive at their destination.
No road rage, drunken drivers
Hinder their arrival;
Bless all speeders' minds with patience.

And if weather hampers me
And forces me to go slower,
I do so knowing it's for my best.
And no foul language
Or feeling of anguish
Will interfere or have me vexed.
I will remain calm and understanding,
Though my time is demanding,
And I know on-time somewhere I should be.
So if late is my arrival,
I will thank God for my survival,
Because though I'm late, He has still blessed me.

As I try to perform the task
In which God has blessed
Me to receive.
My occupation I do unflinching,
Unwavering, to the best
Of my ability.
And though He might have
Something better for me than

This task I now undertake.
I perform it with conviction
'Cause this is my mission
That he's put before me today.

And it's almost a given

Destination

That Satan will mention
The low pay I now receive.
He will tell me to quit
Or get a better job,
But right now, this is where God wants me,
And my light shall not dim,
My joy won't cease,
Despite all the Deceiver says.
I will do what I'm blessed with,
Though daily I'm tested,
But with me my joy will remain.
And I'll receive in due season
My blessing, my right,
So trust him, I will, and wait.
Because God has a plan
For my life, there's a reason—
So in patience I'll pray each day.

Are We to Blame?

As blacks, are we to blame
For the lack of high-paying jobs
In our neighborhoods?
Should we be content
With what we've been lent
And given and still not living good.
When so many of us
Still prefer handouts instead
Of getting out and finding a decent job?
The welfare system is made
To keep us in prison
And has discouraged some of us
From reaching for the top.

As black folks, are we to blame
Because others feel shame for us?
Or disgust because our kids won't pull their pants up.
Thinking that it's cool to look like a fool,
Speaking in broken English
That they've given a name to—Ebonics.
Some feel proud
Because they've given our slang a name.
It's fine when you're on the block,
But when you're on a job hunt, it's
Not received the same.

As black folks, are we to blame
When politicians line their pockets
And leave us broke,
When some of us complain
Instead of getting up and getting out
And casting our vote?
If we utilize our given right,
Liquor stores on our street
Will cease to exist,
Streets would get fixed.
No longer on their campaign trails,
Would we be tricked?

Yes, we are to blame:

Are We to Blame?

If we seek to change things
Without changing our mentalities,
If we fail to teach our kids

How to walk and talk to succeed.
If we don't point out there's good
In everyone,
And at the same time in some
There's greed.

If I want a better future
For me and my family,
It has to start with me.
So if I want things
To change,
We have to stand
Up and let our voices
Be heard so that
It doesn't stay the same:
So are we to blame?

Another Day

My eyes open on another day,
In a place of misery,
A day where you're blessed
If you see another day.
As I dress myself
And I get ready for what may come,
I think it's sad to feel this way,
For someone so young.
Heading to junior high,
What surprises for me wait?
Who knows, because where I live

You're blessed to see another day.

Just last week a friend died
In a drive-by shooting,
Am I next? Is today the day?
Thoughts neither calm nor soothing,
I'm too young to feel this tense
About each car that approaches.
So I stare at each occupant,
On each face I focus.
And when I pass a certain spot
I can't help but look down—
Because blood has stained the concrete
Where my friend was shot down.
Then another car approaches,
Paranoia's all consuming;
It passes without incident
But my heart is still booming.

I manage to make it to the
School house another day without problems
And meet some friends on the way,
Which is probably part of the problem.
But in my neighborhood, friends
Are what keep you alive.
But my friends vary from month
To month because sometimes my friends die—
Like Nikki, who was found

Another Day

Shot in the head point blank,
Just fifteen years old—
On the scene, he was pronounced dead.
Or Mike, who was shot three times
And managed to survive,
Not thanking the good Lord but bragging,
Claiming he can't die.

But in school it's as bad
As it is out on the street,
Because on any given day
You know at least one classmate packing heat.
And fist fights are as common
As the sunrise and sun setting;
And the thought that this
May be my last day breathing is depressing.

But if a problem presented itself,

Survival let me succeed.
But how could I study and make
Good grades knowing someone's watching me!
They're waiting for the day to conclude,
To see if I'm walking alone.
And it's not like I've asked for
This hassle, it's because of the location of my home.
So when the school bell signals
The end with a whistle, my journey home begins.
And as each car passes, I focus on faces,
Not knowing if my life will end.

My Brother's Keeper

Am I my brother's keeper?
Am I responsible for the deeds and misdeeds
And greed that my brother thinks is
His claim to fame?
Am I his voice of reason,
To get him to believe in his talents
And intellect instead of seeking ill-gotten gain?
Should I attempt to educate my brother
And keep him from trouble,
Or would it be in vain?
Because I've already tried
But he doesn't listen: Instead,
He thinks it's all a game.
Should I protect my brother
From the fate he seems
To be running at full speed?
But his speed is slow
Because his baggy pants
Sometimes fall to his knees.

Am I my brother's keeper?
Am I responsible for his failures
And success?
Am I responsible for his clothing
And should I care how my brother dress?
Should I pull his pants up myself
And ask who he's trying to impress?

He tells me women his age
Love the saggy look, dirty drawers and all.
And this is the same man,
After his numerous interviews,
Wonders why jobs never call.
Should I tell my brother
His appearance affects how far
In life he excels,
Not just to go with the flow
Of the status quo, He can be unique and
Still excel.

Am I my brother's keeper?
Should I be held to account

My Brother's Keeper

Because of the words and phrases
That come out of my brother's mouth?
His words degrade sisters
And he tells all who'll listen,
Like he's a racist raised up in the South—
He calls his mothers, grandmothers, and sisters
And cousins yard equipment and female dogs.
He feels proud of degrading
The women who gave him life
And love him despite his flaws.

No, I am not my brother's keeper
Because we are different people
Who strive and live for different things.
Though his actions aren't my actions,
I will try to help him with a passion
Until I pass, but my brother I can't keep.

True Story

I woke up one morning—
Something was wrong.
It's Saturday and something's
Telling me to stay home,
But I didn't listen.
Despite how I feel,
A voice keeps saying,
"Stay home with your kids."
But I took my kids
To their mother's house,
Because I'm going to hit the club
Tonight and show out.
I arrive at her house
And let the kids out of the car,
And kiss them both goodbye
And I hug them both real hard.
They said, "Love you, Daddy,"
Gave me a peck on the cheek.
I love them both so much
It hurts inside when they leave.
And when they're inside
I hit the store to buy some kicks
And a new outfit
To match them with.
But something told me "call Mom
And tell her that you love her."
When I told her that,
She thought I was in trouble.
I told her everything was fine
And hung up the phone,
But the voice kept telling me,
"Jr., go home."
But I didn't listen.
Because tonight is club night,
And once I hit the spot,
Everything will be alright.
And later on at home
I got myself dressed,

True Story

Put on some cologne,
Tonight I'm trying to impress;
But something kept telling me,
"Jr., don't go."
But I still jumped in my car
And hit the road.
Then, later, I was in the club,
Feeling uneasy,
Kind of paranoid
My stomach was feeling queasy.
So I went outside
To get some fresh air
Somebody started fighting—
I just stopped, stood and stared.
There were six guys
Beating up on just one;
They were all laughing
Like they were having fun.
Then a car came and the guy
Getting beat
Jumped in the car
As it sped down the street.
And then the voice said,
"Jr., its time to go.
Get in the car
And get your butt down the road."
But I didn't listen.
Instead, I stayed outside.
Then I heard screaming,
I looked around to see why.
That's when I saw
The guy who was just getting beat,
And he was pointing his AK-47
Right at me.
And then he put the barrel to my chest,
And as he pulled the trigger,
I thought, "Who will raise my kids?
Oh, God!"

What Kind of Man…

What kind of man
Lies to another man
Just to get ahead,

One who would look
You in the eye
And lie about what he said?
What kind of person
Lives a life
Steeped in fear?
The only way they last is by
Lying to their peers.
They wake up afraid of
What will happen today.
No matter what,
I'd do whatever
Just to keep getting paid.
I'm afraid of my boss
Is how they really feel.
For their bosses acceptance,
They breathe and live.
You see it everywhere—
In management,
All up the chain—
People who feel
That hurting people
Is a game.
They go to church like me,
They go to work like me;
The difference is
They don't care
Who they are hurting.
So they're rude
With other people
And think it's their job.
They think tough is needed
But the Devil is in
Their eyes.

What Kind of Man…

They sneak behind
Closed doors and
Backstab their friends
Just to get a promotion,
Then lie about what
They did.
They're snakes and cowards.
They're weasels and fakes.
They'll smile in your face
And lie to you anyway.

These men aren't really men
(They're classified as males)
Because a man does what's right,
Despite what it entails.

So the question is:
What kind of man
Does what's right?
It's probably the man
At peace and with God
In his life.

We Have Been Called

We have been called
Many things, many times,
By those who have tried
To define our very existence
By the minority of us who have
Chosen to commit crimes.
Some feel we all should die,
And we have no right to live
And breathe the same air
As them and their kids.
They feel that we are not in their field
Of prosperity because of how some of us live,
And they think we all cheat, rob and steal.
They watch us on the news and laugh
'Cause TV reports not good, but bad.
They see us on the streets in gangs
And think that we all think the same.
But yet they use no common sense;

Instead, display their ignorance,
Each time they let a sentence slip,
Which proves racism still exists.
But I stand here to prove them wrong,
The ones who sing the same old song.
The ones who hide under sheets and hoods
And think our race isn't any good.
Those who love keeping us in the 'hood,
And would love to kill us if they could.
I stand to let them know one thing:
Me and my family are not suffering,
As well as others of my color,
The hard-working sisters and brothers,
The vast majority, do no wrong,
We work to provide for our homes.
We support causes and benefits
That help the future of our kids.
We march if evil rears its head
And will march until racism is dead.
And those who think we won't succeed
Just need to check our history:

We Have Been Called

We've come from being treated low,
Since then, there's just one way to go.
And to those who like to call us names
And think our future is the same,
I say to you, our future's blessed
With prosperity and great success;
Our kids and grandkids will overcome,
Any hatred with strength, God and love.

We as Parents

We as parents
Have goals and dreams
For our kids to achieve.
We want them to be successful
And to believe they can
Accomplish anything.
That's why we try
To put them in the
Best schools,
And we chastise them
When instead of studying
They act a fool.
We call their teachers
And principals
To find out what's wrong,
Because our child
Has brought a less than
Perfect grade home.

And not a week goes by
That we don't try
To motivate them for greater things,
A pat on the back
For a job well done
When done can achieve many things.
We try to steer them clear
Of pitfalls in life—
That's why we tell them: "Say no to drugs."
We know all of their friends
So we can put distance
Between our kids and thugs.
And we tell them of God,
His son and the cross
So our child's soul will not

Be lost.

We teach them the way,
And teach them to pray,
And do what's right, despite the costs,

We as Parents

So when our child grows
Inside, we will know
That we gave this child everything—
The tools to succeed
And in God to believe,
And with him they can do anything.

These steps to follow
Start today, not tomorrow,
Because our kids are getting older.
It's never too late
To change their direction—
Start now, Hell's not getting colder.

We as Black People

We as black people
Have lost our language
And our individuality.
From the day we arrived in boats,
And were sold
Like pieces of someone's property.
Brothers and sisters,
Husbands and wives, separated,
To make someone profit.
In barns and stores demeaned,
We were sold and explored
Not like humans but objects.

We were taught another language,
Beat into submission
And, branded to them, we were cattle.
To work in the fields
Day and night we lived for their purpose;
To them, that's all that mattered.
But our hearts were strong,
Inside we kept songs,
And sung them while working the fields.
And when we got a chance,
We ran for the North
Because we knew this was no way to live.
Some black people made it,
Some kept on trying,
Even though they kept getting caught.
The punishment brutal,
Their attempts seem futile,
But they didn't understand
The black man's heart.

We as black people
Have stood strong and proud
In the face of adversity.
Throughout the years, we've shed tears,
Marched and held hands,
But breaking us they did not succeed.
And though some have worn masks
To hide their faces,

We as Black People

Others have hid in high-up places
In order to spread their hatred.

I stand here today to say
They did not succeed.
With the heart of a warrior
Polished from years of battle,
I stand today and say that we will not retreat.
Today we demand equality
For us and our families
And this, one day, we will achieve.
If it means we march through the streets
Generation after generation,
Until we witness hatred's defeat,
We as black people,
We will not retreat.

Two Voices

We all have two voices
That talk to us on
A daily basis:
One voice speaks truth
And the other voice
Speaks hatred.
And as believers,
We should turn away
From the Deceiver,

The voice that leads to
Damnation, death
And eternity with unbelievers.
So we should stand steadfast
And say, "Satan, get behind me,
'Cause this vessel is
A Holy One and my
Creator resides inside of me."

One voice would say
The choice you've just made
Is wrong:
"I'd never deceive you;
I'm just here to keep you safe
And strong.
Haven't I helped you time and time again
To tell off all your foes?
Haven't I shown you pleasure
In the past with people
You didn't know?
Haven't I brought you
Money frequently
From playing the lottery?
Why would I deceive you?
You know you mean
So much to me."

And the other voice
Would simply say:
"I died for your sins,
And despite his deception,

I'm here for your protection;
I'll be with you till the end."

So both of these voices
Provides us with choices,
And which choice would we grasp—
Either the voice of the Deceiver,
Or the One who died for our sins?

To My Kings And Queens

To my black queens: Life is hard enough.
To begin,
Don't lie down and have kids
Just to keep a man.
Don't fall for the game
That these shysters play.
When they come, throw them
A stick and they'll run away.
Keep your legs closed and have goals
And big dreams.

Don't fall for the slick lines and nice things
That men use to abuse and take
What you've got.
Self respect will stop
Any plans they plot.
Once you give away your innocence,
It's gone forever.
AIDS is real, even if he's
Handsome and clever.
He could give you two things
That you just can't shake—
AIDS or kids, so think,
Don't make a mistake.

If he ain't willing to wait,

You should send him away;
But if he's true, he can
Wait until your wedding day.
Your body is yours—when they
Ask, just say no.
If there's no ring, there's
No fling, and you've got to go.

To my black king, my son,
Who carries my name,
Who wears my face,
And my blood flows through your veins:
Women are to be loved, hugged
And given respect.
They're not punching bags

To My Kids

Because you wanna keep them in check.
How would you feel if someone
Beat the women you loved?
Keep your hands to yourself
And lift up your head;
Real men defend women from
Cowards who beat them.

A strong black male
Knows how to treat them.
There's nothing wrong with
Opening doors, pulling out chairs.
There's nothing wrong with
Leaving when your temper flares;
You come back when you're
Relaxed and no longer mad.
There is no reason to hit
Her, even if you're mad.
You control your hands
Your mouth, your legs, get out.
If you feel you want to swing,
Pack your bags and bounce.
Don't get caught up in a jail cell
Cursing and fussing.
Be a strong black man—
Leave before you touch her.

To Royalty.

The Fall

The last thing I remembered
Was yelling and screaming—
Then no noise at all.
Everywhere there was black;
At the end of a tunnel was light
Then I began to fall.
Faster and faster
I yelled and screamed,
Hoping something would slow my descent.
I tried to pray
But was it too late,
Even for me to repent.

And slowly the temperature changed…
Below I saw flames
God, that must be Hell!
The closer I got,
I felt intense hot
And the louder I screamed and yelled.
And at that moment,
I remembered all of the
People I did wrong:
I remembered my kids
And even my wife
Who cried nights when I didn't come home.
"My kids, oh God, my kids!" I thought,
As the flames came closer and closer.
I've wasted my life
Not doing what's right
And now my life is over.
My skin burned in flames,
This wasn't a game,
And I tried to cry.
I begged God, "Please,
Give me another chance.
I promise that I will live right."

Then my eyes opened,
I yelled in my room,
My wife said it was a dream.
Then I told her I was

The Fall

On my way to Hell
But I begged God to please,
Give me one more chance—
And that's what he granted.
Then I got down on my knees,
I repented and asked God for forgiveness.
Now my life is right:
I do right by all
Because of that fall
That happened to me that night.

The Emptiness

There was a hole deep
Inside of me no one could fill.
I tried to fill the void

With alcohol but it stayed, still.
I tried to fill it with people,
Friends and family.
But something was missing
I felt deep inside of me:
When I was out
In the clubs, I felt something was wrong;
I felt out of place
So many times I went home,
And stared at the ceiling,
Thinking there has to be more
Because this emptiness,
I need to know what it's here for.

Is it sadness, anger
Or some kind of anxiety?
Inside I'm feeling I'm missing
Something important to me.
So I say to myself,
"In my life, what's missing?"
Then a voice said something to me
But I didn't listen.
Then I said, "Is it women
Money or even fame?
Is my conscience telling me
I have caused someone pain?"

Then that voice said to me:
"Son, you're missing me.
I have been here all along,
Waiting patiently,
Knocking on your heart
For you to let me in.
I'm all you need
Because I'm me, you can depend."
Then I said, "Yes,
Jesus, fill my heart and soul."
Now that emptiness
I had is there no more.

Temptations

Lord, help me; my flesh is weak
And temptations abound.
If I've ever needed your guidance,
I need it now.
I need a word from you
To plant in my heart,
Because on this day, doing the right thing
Seems real hard.

At times my mind wanders

On things unclean,
And my flesh hungers for things
Not right for me.
The temptations come in forms of
Food or lust,
So each day I have to pray
Because it's you I trust.

So this day, Lord, please
Help me control my feet.
And this day, Lord, please
Help me control what I eat.
And Lord, please help me
Control my hands and mouth,
So in your name I will
Stand strong and stout.
So when the Devil brings
Temptation in
I just rebuke it.
In your name, I claim
Any temptation fruitless.

Sunset

The sun sets on another
Day you've made
And one I was blessed to see;
And throughout the struggles
And different situations,
I've kept your words inside of me.

When either my kids,
My friends or my enemies
Have brought me pain,
A song of praise
Inside of me all day
I sang.

When I received a bill
The Devil said that
I couldn't pay,
I gave the bill to you
And let you have

Your way.

When my boss
Tried to give me a hard time
And cause me grief,
I just smiled
And preformed the duty
In which you've assigned me.

And as this day now comes to an end,
I'd say it was a good day
'Cause you made the sun shine
And came right on time:
So to you I say thanks.

Statistics

I was supposed to be a statistic:
Born in an age of poverty and shame,
Born to a broken family,
Middle kid of seven—would anyone
Remember my name?
Would anyone think this lost soul
Would prevail and excel,
Despite what his parents were told?
A heart murmur would be
His downfall; he'll be lucky
If he gets old;
And on top of that, he's black
And statistics say he'll end up
In jail.

Like so many other sisters and brothers
Whose dreams they've
Slowly derailed.
I was supposed to be a statistic
Even before I turned fifteen.
I was supposed to have a record
Is what they claimed on TV.
And despite my living conditions
And friends going to prison,
I somehow kept my nose clean.

Not saying I didn't have my share
Of run-ins with the law,
I was blessed God watched over me.
And knowing every day death
Was a gunshot away,
I myself believed what they said;
Between loud ambulance sirens
And best friends dying,
Would I end up dead?

But as weeks led to months,
And months led to years,
Each birthday I thought brought me closer.
To the end results of their statistics
Because they said I wouldn't get any older.

Statistics

I was supposed to be a statistic
And even though I proved
The statistics untrue,
They tell me my son might be
A statistic, regardless of anything
That I do.
They say move out the 'hood,
Raise him up right and he
Still might end up behind bars
Or strung out on crack
Just because he's black—
That's why each day I gave him to God.

And statistics: despite everything,
It doesn't mean me and my son
Will be a statistic.
So I put my faith in God,
Because statistics are flawed
And only He knows the
Real ending.

Saying "Whatever"

Sometimes I feel like
Saying "whatever"
To my current situation,
Giving up, throwing in the towel
And leaving it all for a vacation.
It's only when I'm tested
That I feel like giving up
And walking away.
But Mamma didn't raise a quitter
So I stay to fight
Another day.

Sometimes I feel like
Saying "whatever"
When I'm at work working hard,
Because my boss is pressing
My nerves, looking over my shoulder,
And he won't stop.
If I went with my first mind,
I would turn around
And give him a piece of mine.
Tell him to take this job
And shove it
And that he's interfered for the last time.
But I stay relaxed
And finish my task
And try to hold my peace,
Although I want to
Take this mouse and shove it
Where he can't see.

Sometimes I feel like
Saying "whatever"
And dragging my spouse to court,
And make her pay
For all the days
She made this marriage hard;
For every time she fussed
And complained

Because of the toilet seat;
Or because my shoes and socks

Are not in the spot
They're supposed to be;
Or because she wants to talk
And talk only when
I'm watching the game.
But I love my wife,
She's part of my life,
So I press on and stay.

Sometimes I feel like
Saying "whatever"
And putting my kids in a home,
Let someone adopt them,
Feed them and hopefully
They'll leave me alone.
They eat all the food
And dirty the house
And think it's no big deal.
They break my furniture
And talk back.
They forget to feed the
Dog and cat.
They refuse to make
Good grades in school.
They sneak out the house
Sometimes at two.
They've stolen the car
To go to clubs,
And all of their friends
Are nothing but thugs.
They think that money
Grows on trees;
They steal out my wallet
When I'm asleep.
They lie to me, lie to me,
All the time,
And I think that one's
Involved in crime.

But despite all of
Those things, I just
Can't say "whatever"

To them.
So now when I
Wanna say "whatever,"
I pray and pray
That it'll get better.
So I won't give up, no,
Not ever,
Even though I feel
Like saying "whatever."

Prosperity

I've tried many things
To achieve fortune and fame.
They offered the same
Lies and over-exaggerated
Fairy tale endings:
Open an eBay store
And make money from the beginning;
Or make cash while you sleep

And receive checks in the mail;
No work involved, problem solved,
You're guaranteed to excel.

You see them on TV,
Living the life of the rich,
Eating the finest foods
And driving expensive whips.
They tell you that you can do it—
Just send them a check
And in no time you'll have
Fame, fortune and respect.

I've lost hundreds of dollars
And fell for a number of schemes
All in the pursuit of happiness,
Money and dreams.
It's funny what one will do
To make a dollar or two;
I was sold false dreams
That would never come true.
But then I learned
That success rarely happens overnight:
It takes commitment
And persistence, nothing to be taken light.

Now with God, hard work
And patience, I will succeed.
In His time, He will grant me
My prosperity.

My Son

My life changed this day
When I my firstborn
Opened his eyes.
I didn't realize
I'd be blessed
With such a wonderful surprise.
I didn't know I could
Love someone this much
'Cause we just met;
My protégé, baby boy,
This day I'd never forget.

When he let out his first yell,
I felt compelled to hold
Him tight.

My life changed
For the better,
I had to get myself right.
I made myself a promise
As I watched him go to sleep:
That I would be the best father
A man could be.

That he would never go hungry
As long as I could work.
And I'd protect him
With my life
'Cause that's what he deserved.
And I would protect him
From all who would
Do him harm.
And when he ever felt sad,
My shoulder he could cry on.

That he'd get the best
Education his father
Could afford,
Even if it meant
Working two jobs,
Despite if it got hard.

My Son

And I told him
One day he would
Grow up to be a man,
And though not being perfect,
I'll raise him the best
That I can.

As I watched him sleep
With his thumb in his mouth,
Little hands and little feet,
I wondered what he dreamt about:
Was he afraid like me
Or was he sleeping in peace?
I prayed over my son
As I watched him breathe:
I prayed it would never cease
And that he's blessed
With increase;
And I prayed,
Hoping my son could
Be the best man he could be.

My Mind

My mind tells me at times
I'm not capable of success and I feel stressed.
Many people I wanna impress,
But nevertheless I press.
To achieve my goals
While fighting negativity
That comes in droves.

When I take one step,
Something knocks me back;
It's just me fighting myself
So I got to relax.
Take it a day at a time,
While getting away from these naysayers
And player haters
That seems to pop up everywhere.
From my family and friends,
Who seek my dividends,
They want my money to end
So they all can laugh again,
And point fingers and say they told me that I wouldn't succeed,
Keep me on their level,
But ain't no Devil stopping me.
Let me repeat it again:
Ain't no Devil stopping me—
I will be all I can be.

As long as there is breath in me,
I will fight the good fight.
Despite what it looks like,

Despite what's in my path,
I will succeed to great heights.
I have seen the dream
That's been promised to me.
So despite what my mind
And my friends and family
Say to me, I will succeed.

My Hero

The strongest woman I ever met
Was most of the time stressed.
Raising seven kids, working full time,
At my young age, I was still impressed.
From my earliest memory
Of her trials while raising me,
From dealing with a man
Who spent more time in the streets
Than with his own family.

I remember her silent tears
From the pain of many years
Of being mistreated,
But she always prayed
Because with God she'd beat it.
And after years of unhappiness,
She was left alone to raise
Her seven kids,
And attend college to obtain
A degree.

I still remember the days
She sat at the table studying.
I remember thinking to myself,
"You have a job, you don't need school.
You work all day, study at night—
That's something I wouldn't do."
But she taught me a valuable lesson,
A lesson to this day I still take seriously:
That despite your age, if you have goals
You need to keep learning to succeed.
But you have to understand,
She was raising seven kids, one badder than the next.
But she received her degree,
Which was amazing to me, and I gained
A new level of respect.

And now that her kids are grown

And gone from her shelter,
She still studies for her future

My Hero

So it can be better.
Now, everyone has someone
In their life
That they consider their hero.
My mom is my hero,
The lady who loved me
From the age of zero.

My Fault

Is it my fault that I was brought
Into a world of hatred and disdain,
That in my mind the only way to gain
Was to cause pain?
And without guidance and simple direction,
I was forced to lean on drug dealers
For protection.

Is it my fault that my mom,
Despite all of her time
And daily discussions,
She couldn't
Stop her baby boy from hustling?
And throughout the years, I was influenced
By peers who lived with no fears,
And even my older brother, who I looked
Up to, was always in trouble.
What man would step in
And stick out his hand
And explain things to me in ways I'd understand?
But no one explained that life in the game
Would lead to me wearing chains,
Having a number for a name.

Is it my fault that my record
Is as long as Texas
And finding a job now
Is greatly affected?
Should I tell them about my incarceration
On my application
And hope they show kindness and patience?
Now wishing I would have listened
To older folks when they told me to stop tripping.
They told me to stay in school
And get a degree,
But back then those things I felt
Didn't apply to me.

Yes, it's my fault
That I chose a path of destruction,
A day of hustling over doing
Something constructive.

My Fault

Knowing it's my fault for my life,
Could I influence those like me to do right?
Could I influence young brothers on the block
Carrying Glocks to take a minute and stop,
And learn from my mistakes and bad decisions
And stay out of prison?

Yes, it's my fault,
But accepting responsibility
Still doesn't change my reality.
It doesn't change my present situation
Or my future salary.
No education,
My future I'm facing
Seems dark with no light at the end.
Can I succeed where others have failed,
Become a statistic again?
But I am here today to tell you
I have succeeded so far,
But the first step was realizing
That my life, is my fault.

Inspiration

I waited for this day
So long, to be with the one
Of my dreams.
I knew the first day
I saw you that you
Would marry me.
I remember seeing
Your pretty smile
And thinking, "How beautiful!"
Before you said a word
To me, I knew that
I would fall in love.

We talked and talked,

Quickly friends we became.
You told me of your dreams,
Your hurt, your pain,
How the last man hurt you
And treated you wrong,
We talked all day
And all night long.
It was hard for you to trust another man again,
So we took it slow
To let you know I understand.
That those others
Have hurt you
But I won't cause you pain.
As long as I am with
You, you won't need
Another man.

We got to know each other,
We told our fears.
I held you close to me
At times when you shed tears.
We talked about
Our future, and
We'd be together
Through problems
Through thick and thin,
No matter the weather.

Inspiration

Your smile made me blush,
Your touch made me shiver.
When I thought of you
My heart would quiver.
When your name was
Mentioned in your absence,
I'd smile.
When I heard your voice
Over the phone, I'd smile.
And when you said
You were coming,
I felt like a child,
Eager for your arrival,
My heart
Would go wild.

But now on this day,
You will be my wife,
My daily inspiration,
The center of my life.
I looked you in the eyes
In front of the judge

And God,
And promised to love
You and never do
You harm;
For rich and poor,
Either healthy or sick,
For good or bad,
No matter how
Hard it gets.
You promised me
The same as you
Let a tear fall;
We were joined
As one with
God above all.

We kissed, we kissed,
It was like July the Fourth.
The night we spent

Inspiration

Was something
I could not have planned for.
And since that day,
Ever since that time,
You have been an inspiration
To my life.

I Will Not Cede

I will not cede to my enemies
Of what's right and just;
And though they come ready for battle,
I stand 'cause in God I trust.

I will not cede to the naysayer
And negative people in my path;
Though they be family or friends,
In the face of doubters I laugh.
And though the wind blows fiercely
Against the sails of my life, to throw me off course,
I know that nothing can stop me
From reaching my appointed shore.
My armor and shield stands before me
To repel all advances,
So with Him on my side,
In this or any other battle, I like my chances.

I will not cede, knowing
I have the maker of all things great and small
As my protector and healer,
And with his blessing I shall not fall.
I will succeed, not cede, each day
As I face the enemy.
I will be confident and strong
'Cause that's what God has put in me.
And I will love all and seek refuge
In Him who forever has my gratitude.

And while there's breath in me,
I will not cede; despite Satan's magnitude,
I will press on.

I Sit Amongst Bills

I sit amongst bills,
Past due notices,
And none I can pay;
A man too proud to ask for
Handouts but bills need to be paid.
Pride can't feed my family
Or put clothes on my kids backs.
The stress I'm feeling daily
Makes it hard for me to relax.

I've looked for job after job,
No luck finding employment.
I feel like a failure to my family
And in my heart there is torment.
And every week I'm down on myself,
Thinking the best I can do
Is unemployment checks.
Though my wife says she believes
In me, it's hard for me to
Believe in myself.

Am I not saying the right things
While I'm in these interviews?
Is it the color of my skin,
My haircut, my pants, my shoes?
Do I have bad breathe
Or show a lack of confidence?
Or do they think I'm unqualified
I lack experience?

Is what I think
As the bills are laid out before me,
I just have to believe in God
And pray my phone will ring.
Ring!

I Apologize

I've sinned in the past
For many different reasons,
And for that, Lord, I apologize.
I've tried ungodly ways
To make money, and not waiting
For my reason,
For that, Lord, I apologize.
I've let ungodly words
Come from my mouth at times;
For that, Lord, I apologize.
And in my youth against
Your Ten Commandments,
I've committed crimes;
For that, Lord, I apologize,
I've sang songs
That degrade your children,
Failed to modify
The way I'm living,
Took too many chances
At going to prison;
For that, Lord, I apologize.
I've taken property
That I didn't pay for;
For that Lord I apologize.
You've blessed me immensely
But still I complain more;
For that, Lord, I apologize.
And on this day, I strive
To do my best,
Despite the evil forces
That will come to test
My heart, and desire to
Do what's right
And do what's
Pleasing in your sight.
And despite it all,
I'll stand and claim,
That I have power
In your name,

I Apologize

To resist all negatives
That come my way.
And if I shall stumble,
This day I pray,
Lord, forgive me—
Because I know what's right
And with a humble heart,
I apologize.

Hurt

Can I get past
The hurt and pain this day,
That totally engulfs me on the inside?
Can I feel happiness again
And not depression,
Which lessens my quality of life?
And though I cry inward
And out loud because of this wrong
That has visited me,
The person that I used to lean on
Is the one who has
Deceived me.

The pain that I am feeling,
Will its magnitude ever decrease?
Because it so engulfs me

That I whimper at night
While I'm asleep.
And though I'm told it will
Get old, now it doesn't
Seem so,
Because the pain
Has seemed to invade
My heart, my mind, my soul.

Each day I seek encouragement
Because discouraged at times
I am,
Until I remember
To whom I belong, whose property I am.
So with my Bible open,
(His words I quoted and repeated every verse)
Now I'm at peace—
My pain, my loss,
Is behind me; there's no longer hurt.

Go to Church

I work all day, head hurts
From my job.
My boss keeps picking on me
And he won't stop.
There are not enough hours
In a day to do the work,
And I was planning on
Leaving early to go to church.
So I put my head down
And tries to get busy,
And when I think I'm done
They bring me more work to finish.
But looking at my watch,
I don't have much time,
And my boss is telling me
I've got a deadline.
And on top of that
My kids keep ringing my phone,
Asking what I'm gonna cook tonight
When I get home.
So now I'm juggling
Phone calls and my work.
And, looking at the time,

I will be late for church.

But with hard work
I finish all the work on time.
I meet my deadline,
Now it's time to unwind
And go to church—
That's just what I need.
But the traffic is worse
Than I've ever seen;
Bad car wreck,
Eighteen wheeler flipped on its side.
But, Devil, you ain't winning—
I'm a make church tonight.
Come Hell or high water,
I will make God's house.
So, Devil, you're a lie,
I proclaim it from my mouth.

Go to Church

Then the traffic lightens up
And I'm a little late,
But it's all worth it to
Hear what the man of God has to say:
Now I'm at peace.

Freedom

We were slaves took from our land,
Shackled off in a boat.
We weren't treated like human beings,
We were just cargo,
Husbands and wives separated
Just to be someone's slave.
All didn't make it: Some
Are lying in the sea as their grave.

When we came over, we were sold
Like cattle and pigs;
Families were split,
Going to the highest bid.
Black slaves who didn't obey
Were beat or killed;
The others spent all day
Working in the cotton fields.

Many escaped to the North
Where the blacks were free.
Many were tried and hung
For their attempts to flee.
Many of our black women
Were raped and sodomized.
We were lower than animals
Off in the slave masters' eyes.
They killed and maimed us
If we knew how to read,
So don't forget how it started
And how our people were treated—
So many died so you can have a chance at freedom.

After the Civil War, they freed us
But continued to beat us.
We continued marching
And voicing our rights as black people.
We shouldn't go to the back
Of the bus, we're not second-class.
We were attacked by evil men

Who wore hoods as masks.
In our schools we weren't

Given the things we need.
They tried their best to
Make it hard for us to succeed.
We were stalked by the Klan,
Harassed, intimidated.
Jim Crow was alive,
They kept us segregated.

Martin Luther King marched
And sang *We Shall Overcome*.
Malcolm X demanded respect,
He wasn't dumb.
We had strong leaders to lead us
Through a time of struggle.
We wouldn't be defeated, we demanded
Justice out of trouble.
Through the boycotts and sit-ins,
We wouldn't be denied.
Equality for everybody
And not just one side.
So don't forget how it started
And how our people were treated—
So many died
So we could have a chance at succeeding.

There is still racism living
Off in two thousand and six:
We're denied opportunities
That other people get;
We get longer jail sentences
For the same infraction.
We still march in Washington,
And demand action.
Things have gotten better
But we have a long way to go:
When equalities are given
Without a need for quotas;
When Martin Luther King's dream
Is followed by all;
When we're all treated the same

And not like dogs.
But us young people, at times,
Forget what's been achieved—

From slavery to being the person
You wanna be.

And the struggle ain't over:
We just have to learn from our past.
Make sure our people
Didn't die in vain
Now is our chance.
To take up the cause
And never pause, not for a second.
Keep the dream alive
And fight to be heard and respected.
So don't forget how it started
And how our people were treated,
So many died so we can have a chance at freedom.

Depression: Part 1

Is happiness a figment
Of my imagination?
I've been unhappy for so long;
For life I've lost motivation.
Getting out of bed seems
To be a heavy chore for me,
So I instead stay in bed,
Eat and watch TV.

I've been told my actions
Are in line with depression,
But in my mind my actions
And depression—there's no connection.
I try and remember a time
When joy was in me,
When I greeted every day
With praise a plenty.
It's hard to go back that far
But I feel in time this will pass;
One day I will be cried out,
Surely this won't last.

My job I've probably lost,
My boss is tired of excuses.
He tells me to get counseling
But I feel his advice is stupid.
Though I feel sick every day,
And my friends have stopped calling
(I think I've run them all away).

My family has tried to help
Though I've told them I needed none.
But they've tried for so long
And even my kids say I'm no fun.
My spouse tries to help out
And tries to stop me from crying;
My spouse tells me I'm crazy
Whenever I talk about dying.
And I've gained thirty pounds
Just eating and sleeping all day.

Depression: Part 1

My spouse tries to touch me
But each time I push my spouse away.
For my life has little purpose
And to me a bleak outlook.
I went in my drawer to get a gun
But instead I found a book.

Depression: Part 2

This book said I was loved,
Although I felt no one cared;
This book said someone loved me,
Every single hair.
Then I read the story of Job
And how he lost it all,
But he put his trust in God
And his faith did not fall.
And God rewarded him with more
Than he had before,
And I thought, "If God can bless him,
Then what am I crying for?"

Then I read the whole chapter
Of the greatest love story ever told,
How Jesus Christ died
And that his death was foretold.
He made blind men see,
He made the lame walk;
He made the dead awaken
And people came just to hear him talk.
I read how he was betrayed
And how he forgave his captors,
How nails were put in his hands and feet
And he died shortly after.
After three days he rose

And sat on God's right side,
In Heaven with the Father,
And it's where he now resides.
And that his holy spirit
Was sent back down to earth,
And that accepting him in your life
Is having a rebirth.

That's when I put down the book
And got on my knees,
And asked him to come into my life
And reside inside me.
He came in and changed my life,
Each day for the better;
Now I'm no longer sad
Or unhappy because God is my Shepherd.

Come On

I still remember it
Like yesterday…

A voice told me,
"Go down right away."
It was Sunday morning
And altar call,
And a voice kept saying,
"My son, come on."
But I was afraid
Of what people would say,
And I was too
Deep in sin anyway—
"How could he forgive me?"
Is what I thought.

But the voice kept on saying,
"My son, come on."
So I told myself, "Next time
I will give my life."
The voice said to me,
"Now is the time,
And another day is promised
To no one,
So come on, I've been
Waiting, my son."

So I stood up
And looked around,
And told myself
I was going down.
I thought to myself,
"What if people laughed

And I'd lose all the friends
That I have?"
But the voice said to me
"I would give you more,
So come, my son,
What are you waiting for?"

So I took one step

Come On

Out in the aisle
While the pastor said,
"Come on down."
Then another step,
My heart was beating fast;
Then another step,
I let my doubts past.
Then I could visualize
Jesus with opened arms,
And saying, "Just a few more
Steps, my son."

And then I ran to
My Savior's embrace,
And I've been held
By him since that very day.
So Jesus is telling
You to come on,
Run to him today—
He will welcome you home.

Baby's Daddy

Deep down inside,
A searing pain I tried to hide,
After being told that the baby
That I now hold isn't mine.
The little hands and feet
And eyes that looked up at me
Match another man's description
And will hold no traits of my identity.

The pain that shot through me
Nearly blew me out of my shoes,
And after that came the agony,
Depression, rage, then the blues.
I've been waiting for this baby
For nine months; call me crazy,
But at this time I want to choke,
Choke, choke this lady.
But instead I stayed calm
And told myself I'd do no harm
To this lady because I knew
One day her uppance would come.

But that didn't ease the pain,
My embarrassment or my shame,
And what made the situation
Worse was that the baby's daddy walked in.
Smiling like it was a joke,
A confrontation he tried to provoke,
But instead of losing my head
I smiled and said, "Later, we'll talk, bro."

I refused to let them see my pain
Even though she was smiling again,
And the baby was smiling, playing,
This night my clean record might get stained.
But instead I put the baby down
Turned around and walked out,
And thought, "No child support"—
There is a silver living to this cloud.

At Times, I Contemplate

At times, I contemplate

On how life would be
If my grandparents
And great-grandparents
Didn't stand up for me…

If they didn't endure
Water cannons and vicious dogs,
Constant humiliation
By the officers of the law.

At times, I contemplate,
Even meditate on, my current situation
And think it can't compare
To what my parents were facing…

The constant name-calling,
Arrests and detentions
Just because of their skin pigment…

Treated like scum of the earth
By those who claim to love God
(Even though they've never seen him),
But show hatred, disrespect and viciousness
Toward God's people.

At times, I contemplate,
When I'm sitting in a restaurant
And a white waiter brings me a meal,
If my great-grandparents
Were alive today
They'd think this was a big deal…

Because they had to fight
Just to get served
And just to take a seat so they could eat
In any restaurant they chose.
So they sat in droves
Just to let the world know
That racism, they would defeat.

At Times, I Contemplate

At times, I contemplate:
If there was no civil rights movement
Could I live wherever I pleased?
And I contemplate: if Martin Luther King
Never had a dream,
Would my black kids have white kids
As friends and sit in class together;
Ride in the front of the bus together;
Stand shoulder to shoulder

To face whatever?

At times, I contemplate!

First of the Month

Lord, grant me the strength,
The knowledge and courage
To proceed and succeed on this day,
Because when your help it's possible
To overcome any obstacle
And you are only a prayer away.

On this first day today,
I prepare mentally for my challenge
In this month that is sure to come.
And though I'm but your humble servant,
And I am not perfect,
When anger arrives, I will not succumb,
To any temptation: I will stand
And be patient
And wait on your intervention.
I will look to the hills

Because I know you will
Quiet all my month-long dissension.
My armor and my shield,
In your book is my plan
On how I'll tackle each day.
I say, "Satan, get the behind me!
I seek peace and prosperity
And God will lead the way!"

So on this first day,
I do feverishly pray:
Lord, please order my steps,
'Cause though the road is long,
With you I'll stay strong,
And this month you I won't forget.

The Grave

There's more talent
In this one place than any other.
This place is filled with talent;
Now, no words are uttered.
This place is filled with
The dreams and hopes never fulfilled.
In this place, great minds,
Unused, succumbed to fears.
In this place, there are leaders
Who never stepped forth.
In this place, great minds
Deteriorate, leaving generations poor.

There are great voices
Never used like God intended.
There are artists and poets
Who never used what God had given.
There are great speakers
And great dreams left undone.
In this place, poverty succeeded
Because fear had won.
This place that I speak of
Is one you pass each day.
This place is where
Dreams go to die:

This place is the grave.

I Will March

I will speak for those
Who feel they don't have a voice.
I will fight for those
Who have been persecuted,
For this is my choice.
I will march through the streets
Singing *We Shall Overcome*.
And like so many before me,
I will march until we've won.

I will march until
All God's children
Are on even scale.
I will march hand-in-hand,
Despite the cost it entails.
I will march through the
Snow and rain until my goal's achieved.
I will march with
Many different races
Who seek equality like me.

I will march until
Dr. Martin Luther King's
Dreams are fulfilled.
I will march through
The lowest valley and
Up the highest hill.
And while on the quest
To do what's just,
For all who have suffered in their plight,
As God is my witness I will march
Until what is wrong is made right.

Our Destination

I hide in the darkness,
Waiting with others
Who seek freedom like me.
We hide cluttered, close,
Sleeping in shifts
To reach the land where
Negroes are free.
At times we hear sounds
Of shuffling feet
Or horses galloping by.
And since we are slaves,
We quietly pray
That no one knows we are nearby.
We are so close
And yet so far.
Tomorrow we shall reach the state
Where all Negroes are free
To live how they please;
For that moment, we can't wait.
We know there's a price
To capture us all—
We are wanted dead or alive.
There are six in all
And we are led by
Harriett Tubman so we will survive.
We left the plantation
And we know we are facing
Death or mutilation.
But we can't turn back
So forward we move—
Because freedom is our destination.

I Vow

Last year I vowed
To do better than this;
I will be more successful
For the last next year I wished.
My resolutions just keep on
Being the same:
Please, Lord, bless me abundantly
With wealth, prosperity and fame.

But last year I vowed
To make this year better.
I even quoted it daily
And put my wishes in letters
To friends and family,
Asking them to pray for me,
That in all I try
That I will succeed.
It was like a resolution
I was supposed to keep
But my life hadn't changed—
Is it because of me?

I vowed to have a better job
But my job is the same.
I vowed to be serious,
And don't play life as a game,
But yet again I'm doing things
Like life is a joke.
I vowed no more cigarettes
But I still secretly smoke.
I vowed no more profanity,
No cursing and such,
But when I'm in traffic
I still, at times, slip
And cuss.
I vowed to love my family
So much that it hurts
But my patience runs short
And it's made my anger,
Much worse.

I Vow

So for the new years

The only vow I will make,
Is to thank God daily
For blessing me awake.
My vow will be to seek
Him first and let him
Order my steps.
Because with him
Change is possible.
So praising him, I vow
To do my best.
I vow!

www.ingramcontent.com/pod-product-compliance
Lightning Source LLC
LaVergne TN
LVHW050336160826
845677LV00014B/3646

9798847732550